And Other Stories that Came from …Where?

Al DeLucia

Contents

Title	Page
Cold Start	3
Dreamscape #4 – Rite of Passage	4
Hands Part 1	7
El Desvio	9
It Comes to Everyone	14
Freewheeling	15
Dates	15
Quickway	16
Beach Song	17
Assateague	19
Moth Ball Fleet	19
Watermelon	21
Credo et Meno	22
Cold Circle	23
Ya Know What I Mean?	25
The Last Time I Saw Her	28
Proper Placement	28
Now Anything Goes	29

Catchy Tune	30
Manassas	31
The Parable of the Edge 34	
Specie	35
Risk Analysis	36
Airport	37
Layered Learning	38
More on Learning	40
Buddies	40
Diminished Chord	41
Freddie	42
Hands Part 2	46
Pay Attention to What You Are Doing	47
What's It All About?	48
Nellie	50
Aunt Jo	53
First Draft Lottery	53
2nd Amendment	54
Dick Street	55
Times Square	56
Years Later…	57
Bailey Hall	58
283	58
Elmer	60

My Right Side	~~61~~ 63
Arthur	~~63~~ ~~65~~
Drips	64 66
Johnstown	~~65~~ ~~66~~ 67
July 4, 2010	~~66~~ ~~67~~ 68
Three Rules	~~66~~ ~~67~~ ~~68~~ 69
Lake Being	~~67~~ ~~68~~ 69
Ultimate Reality?	~~69~~ ~~70~~ 71
Poem Writer	~~70~~ ~~71~~ 72
La Mia Ora Speciale	~~71~~ ~~72~~ 73
In Cerca di Michelangelo	~~72~~ ~~73~~ 74

Amazon.com

Rev. 72

Cold Start

It was still dark, and it was cold. God, it was cold. Pulling his collar tight, he turned the corner into the wind.

Through the early morning darkness, the truck's cab emerged above the other cars. He liked that about the truck. It was a good truck, but hard to start when it was cold.

He wanted to get the truck running for company.

The choke was broken, so he lifted the air cleaner and sprayed starting fluid into the mouth of the carburetor. The battery had been low, so he knew he had two tries -- three at the most.

He pushed in the clutch to minimize drag on the engine, pumped the gas twice and held it to the floor. He twisted the key. It turned over, kicked once, then died.

"Bitch," he said.

Again, he gave it shot of starting fluid. Again, he pressed the clutch, softer this time, and pumped twice while twisting the key.

It kicked once, and then kept kicking as he kept pumping to keep her going. Then she settled into a steady rhythm and he knew he had her. "That's it, baby," he whispered.

Satisfied, he leaned back, eased out the clutch, and rolled away.

Dreamscape #4 -- Rite of Passage

He willed himself upward: it wasn't easy. Then, as in a noiseless craft, he hovered motionless above the clouds. Blue sky extended everywhere.

He descended through the clouds and leveled above the brick buildings along the Avenue. Suspended, he watched people walking below.

Then he was in motion again, following the roofs of the boxy black cars up the Avenue. He turned left at the traffic light, passed the old church and followed the street down the hill across the tracks to the dirt in front of the lumberyard.

He passed over the weathered fence and the stacks of lumber beyond to a line of boxcars. Two boys were lying on the roof of a boxcar at the near end of the line. He descended and entered the body of the boy named Frankie.

"Shut up, man," the older boy Nickie was saying. "If you're chicken, go home."

"I ain't no chicken, Nicky."

Frankie's heart pounded against the metal boxcar roof. The old feeling came back; the feeling that he wasn't there -- that the world around him wasn't real. He touched the metal surface to make sure it was.

Frankie looked over the edge of the car and up the receding line. Lumber stacks stood close by on the sides of the line. The boys often had hidden among the stacks when they played in the yard.

At the far end of the line Frankie could see puffs of black smoke from a switching engine. The engine sequentially slammed the hitched portion of the line into a detached car, adding it to the line.

Each time a car was hitched, two jolts traveled along the line, car by car: the first jolt occurred as the slack was squeezed out of the couplings as they slammed together, the second as the newly-hitched car rebounded and the slack was restored. The car the boys were on was still unhitched; it sat separated waiting its turn as the connected line approached.

The boys watched the yardman working his way toward them. He was big, and he looked mean.

"He's getting closer," Nicky whispered.

Their hands clutched crushed limestone ballast taken from the track bed below. Frankie felt his heart pounding. He wanted to flee, but paralyzed his legs.

The yardman was directly below them.

Nicky jumped up and threw his stones. They scattered through the air -- one bounced off the yardman's cap. Then Nicky leaped off the boxcar and disappeared into the stacks. Frankie froze, staring at the yardman.

The yardman looked up, his face red. "You little son of a bitch," he yelled. "When I catch you, I'll break your ass!" and started climbing the ladder of the car.

Frankie jumped up, threw his stones, ran toward the front of the car, reached the edge and leaped toward the oncoming line the instant before it slammed in. He missed and dropped into the gap between the couplings as they came together.

The closing couplings surrounded him and crushed him from his armpits to his waist. The slack returned with the rebound.

Frankie looked up at the sky: white clouds moved past the space between the tall converging walls of the cars.

He willed himself up, then hovered. The yardman was on the roof of the car, staring down into the space between the cars.

Stones were scattered on the roof of the car.

Hands – Part 1

He watched his grandmother stir boiling pears with a wooden spoon. She turned away from the stove, reached up in the cabinet for a tin of flour and poured a small mound of flour on the white porcelain table top.

She fashioned a well in the middle of the mound of flour – it looked like a small volcano. She took two eggs out of the big white refrigerator and broke them into the volcano hole; two yellow eyes stared up at the ceiling. She added salt and olive oil, blended the mixture with a fork, and started kneading with her hands.

As he watched, he sipped from the ginger ale she had given him, mixed with red wine she had snuck from his grandfather's jug. Crumbs from biscotti he had dunked floated in his glass. He continued watching as her hands settled down into a regular kneading motion -- a smooth rhythm that came from years of practice that was stored in the hands.

He looked up at her face and she smiled at him, saying nothing but with her eyes as her hands continued their automatic motion.

He had always been fascinated by hands: hands at rest in different positions, hands gesturing, hands talking. Especially hands working: butcher shop hands, mason hands, carpenter hands, upholstering hands, musician hands, ladies knitting or at sewing machines hands. Hands that after years of doing the same thing developed inner intelligence and moved on their own.

He looked at the faces of the owners of the hands. They showed the same look he now saw on his grandmother's face: the look of being at one with the work; the feeling that comes from learning to do something well and then doing it.

He looked down at his own hands grasping the glass with the wine mixture in it, crumbs floating. He wanted his own hands to do something well; his own face to look like that.

His grandmother finished kneading the dough into a ball, covered it, and placed it aside to rest.

El Desvio

(Bad Hemingway #1)

Crossage stood at the door. To the west, he saw mountains quivering in the distance. Black birds circled against the bright sky in the thermal air currents that rose from the yellow desert floor.

Frank, sitting behind Crossage at a small table, opened another beer. Crossage downed the last of his and grabbed another. He pulled a swig and resumed looking out the door.

"Does it come from the mountains, or opposite – from the east…from the sea?" Crossage asked.

Brightness diffracted around the outline of Crossage's back into the cool adobe darkness of the room and hurt Frank's eyes when he looked up.

"Don't know," Frank replied. "No one knows. It just comes...fast and then it's gone. Every 30 years -- like clockwork."

Crossage kept looking out. The sun was lowering. He thought of when he had first heard of it -- years ago after he left his wife and headed south, taking trains as the people and the language changed along the way.

The last train was a small steam engine with two wooden cars. It climbed through switchbacks; then descended into the desert plains and headed east toward the coast.

The natives in the cars spoke in lowered voices, Spanish words mixed with native dialect. Men on the trains looked down, but the women and the children stared and kept staring long after he looked away.

The train stopped at a small village. Thirsty, Crossage went into a small cantina and met Frank. Frank was drinking and joking with two young native girls. That day, after downing much tequila, Frank had told him about El Desvio.

"Where does everyone go?" Crossage asked, turning from the door.

"Up in the mountains," Frank squinted. "Out of the desert."

"Then it must come from the sea," Crossage continued.

"It don't come from nowhere," Frank grunted. "... suddenly it's just there. That's what the natives say, anyway. The fuckin' natives are scared shitless of it -- cross themselves and hug their children."

Frank went for another beer. This was the last beer; they would soon switch to tequila. They hardly ate anymore-- just cold burritos that the girls brought them in the evenings.

Crossage looked at the bed in the rear of the room where the girls were asleep. They were young -- knew what they were doing, he thought.

"You weren't here for the last one," he stated.

"I only been here 10 years."

Crossage resisted the urge to ask Frank why he was here -- why Frank was waiting. Instead, he continued looking out at the mountains. The birds were gone.

The girls were awake, brushing their hair. Each took a sip of tequila, gargled, and spit it out into the basin.

Sentida's dark straight hair fell over her shoulder -- she turned and stared. Dark eyes. Crossage felt a stir, but turned and looked again at the mountains. Now the air was still.

Sentida got up and held Crossage's back; he felt her breathing against him. They stood awhile, then he pulled away.

"Give me some," he said to Frank, motioning toward the tequila.

Sentida went back to the bed. The girls dressed. Frank poured tequila into glasses. There was some beer left in the glasses: They liked the way it made the tequila foam.

The sun was beginning to set over the mountains.

"Then you've been waiting a long time," Crossage added.

Frank didn't answer.

The girls were dressed, watching the men. Crossage looked at Sentida. Fear was growing in the other girl's eyes.

He again looked out the door. In the still air the light had changed -- a soft greenish glow that seemed to come from inside the air itself.

Sentida approached him again. "Viene El Desvio ahora," she said, looking into his eyes.

"It's coming. I know," He replied.

Sentida hugged his chest, her head to the side, her hair under his nose. They stood together for a while. Then Sentida spoke again.

"Quiero quedarme aqui contigo," she said.

"No. You can't. Go with your people," he replied, turning his head away.

Frank sat -- watching them. The other girl was nervous; she got up and grabbed Sentida by the arm. "Vamanos," she said. Sentida did not move; she held Crossage more tightly.

"Va," Crossage said.

"No," Sentida replied. "…con tigo…"

"Go!" Crossage said, pushing her away. He turned from her and took a swig.

Sentida stood for a moment, looking at him. Then she turned to the other girl and said "Vamanos."

The girls grabbed their bags and ran out. The men heard the old truck turn over and cough to a start.

Frank got up and stood beside Crossage. They watched the truck bounce down the rutted road. The other girl looked back and waved. Sentida looked straight ahead. The sun dropped behind the mountains.

"Man, you are one heartless bastard," Frank said.

It Comes to Everyone

"Two coffees. Black!"

He went up to the counter, and, holding his breath, leaned in between smoking nurses and grabbed the coffees left there. Then he returned, put them down on the table, and sat facing her.

"What will you do…?" he asked her.

She had taught him to play cards: war… solitaire… rummy… 500 rummy; had started him reading: Edgar Rice Burroughs, Jack London, Hemingway. She had tried to teach him to knit-- that didn't take hold. But her music did: She had led him by the hand down to the local record shop to buy *Love Me Tender*.

"I don't know. I haven't been able to think about it,"

They sat in silence sipping their coffees.

The coffees cooled and tasted of Styrofoam, so they trashed the cups and walked out of the cafeteria into the lobby.

He pushed the up button. They waited for the elevator.

A nurse went by pushing a stainless-steel cart full of vials.

Freewheeling

Summer night descended as we headed up Route 17 in the Studebaker truck. We passed Red Apple Rest and turned left up the hill into Orange Turnpike.

We climbed up over the ridge. Uncle Tony put it in neutral, shut the motor, and coasted two miles down into the valley.

Wind whistled by the open window. The brake pedal squeaked.

Dates

He had taken a ball peen hammer and a cold chisel from the barn. Ball peen hammers are heavy -- good for driving a chisel into granite.

Then, he pried a flat stone from the low wall that separated the driveway of uncle Tony's farm from the marsh below, sat on a log in the marsh, and carved "1960" into the rock.

He stares at the strange new "6".

Dates… For years, he had collected 45 records, writing purchase dates on the 45s: Silhouettes, the Rays, 6/24/57 (yellow label, easy to write on); Bye Bye Love, the Everly Brothers, 1/15/58 (a maroon and silver label harder to write on because you had to squeeze the date into the narrow silver part).

The night before, dad, feeling his beers, had let him -- 13 -- drive the porthole Buick down the driveway. He almost drove it off the wall.

Dad's whistle startles him. He jumps up, replaces the stone in the wall, stuffs moss around it, and runs up to the house.

"Coming dad!"

Quickway

The new Quickway was a shortcut to Route 17. My older cousin Bobby and I drove up there in Uncle Tony's new '59 El Camino pickup. I was in shotgun, on a bench seat with no seat belts.

Bobby could be reckless; he had totaled his '57 Ford convertible. But he was smart and good with his hands. One snowy day at the farm my younger cousin Mike and I helped him attach a pair of old wooden skis to a sled. Bobby bent and drilled aluminum strips to form U-brackets to bolt the skis onto the runners.

The sled didn't steer well so we tromped a chute through the deep snow down to the frozen pond. The sled raced down and shot out over the ice to the far edge of the pond where a possum hung by its tail from a branch: dead, frozen-solid pink.

The Quickway was straight, with hardly any traffic. "Hey Al, let's do 100," Bobby laughed.

The El Camino had only six cylinders. The speedometer crept up to 100.

Beach Song

A little girl danced barefoot along the beach. The tide was out. The late afternoon sun reflected sequins on the calm water. An ocean breeze lapped small waves up the sloping sand. The little girl's toes followed the moving contour of the water's edge.

She carried a small plastic bucket in one hand, and swung the other in arcs as she danced along and sang to herself. Her hair swept across her face from her turning motion: sometimes she caught it in her mouth; other times she blew it away with a puff.

When a shell caught her eye, she swept down to grasp it with her free hand and arc it into the bucket.

Further along the beach, a little boy sat building a castle of driftwood and sand. Battlements and a moat surrounded the castle. Shells as knights fought stone mythical monsters. Battle plans evolved. He didn't notice the little girl stopped to watch him play, her song gone.

Feeling her gaze, the little boy looked up. Her eyes were dark -- almost black – as was her hair, which hung motionless now over her shoulders.

He motioned her to come join him. The girl shook her head.

The boy rose and walked towards her. He stopped close to her face; their eyes locked.

Then the girl looked down, moving her eyelids, not her head. He waited, watching her lowered eyelids and longing for the eyes to come back.

The she raised her eyes. She smiled at him and took his hand. Together they danced down the beach. She resumed singing.

The boy was very happy, but he did not hear the song.

Assateague

Jennifer was wearing a light blue jacket with fur fringe around the hood and eating a donut with pink frosting. A heard of ponies surrounded her, biting at the donut.

I used to walk her to school through Philadelphia's Society Hill. Each morning, we took a different route, often discovering a new hidden tree-lined, brick-paved alleyway. We skipped together through Three Bears Park -- trying not to land on the pavement cracks.

Jennifer's big brown eyes looked up out of the moving mass that engulfed her. I reached in. A hoof swooshed close to my face.

Mothball Fleet

Sunday afternoons, we drove up route 9W along the Hudson River, past where it widens into the Tappan Zee and then narrows toward Jones Point. There was no bridge yet over the Tappan Zee – that wasn't built until 1952.

We rounded a bend, and rows of ships came into view: tall bows side by side extending out into the river mist, smaller in the distance, anchor chains at the same angle tight against the current. Liberty Ship ghosts of troop transports.

War was in the '50s background: tanks on flatbed railroad cars pulled by black engines belching smoke, savings bonds called War Bonds, movies about Japs and Krauts. Armistice Day, old men in V.F.W. caps handed out red paper poppies. A Spanish American War veteran, in his dark blue uniform and Rough-Rider hat, was propped up stiff and proud on a Memorial Day float. Our fifth grade teacher got upset when a girl raised her hand and said "Heil !".

The mothball fleet is gone now. The SS Jeremiah O'Brien remains, moored at Fisherman's Wharf in San Francisco Bay. A huge propeller is mounted on a rack in a park on the north side of Vancouver Harbor where many of them had been built during the war. Many were sold to other nations, others scrapped or sunk to create reefs.

Watermelon

A sign in the window of the A&P says "Watermelon 5 ¢/lb." It's hot and I have a nickel in my pocket so I go in.

I wait in line at checkout, then ask the lady for a pound of watermelon. She laughs and shouts "Hey this kid wants a pound of watermelon!" Everybody laughs.

I run out.

Credo et Meno

"What have we learned from them? They try to create truths -- then conflict them. Everything is relative for them. No absolutes. They have lost their centers. No subtle differences," Credo was saying. "Their myths are baseless now," he continued, "they have created a system wherein they do not have to deal with the subtlety of existence, which was what made them human in the first place. They've lost who they are…or were."

"Can they then have gods? Aren't gods absolutes?" Meno asked.

"The Gods of Neuterdom," Credo replied.

"Now you're making up words. That won't do"

"Right. Let's get back to the ship and make our report."

Cold Circle

(Bad Hemingway #2)

"Why are you looking at me like that?" the woman asked.

"I'm not looking at you," the man replied, looking away.

"Yes you are. I can't stand it when you look at me like that."

"Like what?"

"You drive me crazy." The woman got up from the table and walked over to the window.

The man looked at her back. It was a long back. Her arms, thin and white, hung down at her sides out of the sleeveless top she wore. He thought of the Egyptian way she had of moving them when she spoke, bending her hands at right angles and sweeping her long nails through the air. A small purse on a thin strap dropped from her right shoulder. She wore a short skirt and brown sandals. She dropped one sandal and curled her toes as she looked out the window. The man loved her very much and felt remorse for his obtuseness.

He got up, walked behind her, and grasped her arms near her downy shoulders.

"I'm sorry," he said in her ear.

The woman stared out the window. Wrapping his arms around her, the man inhaled the moist warmth of her hair, and stared out at the whiteness that reflected off the beach. Native children played on the sand. Boats shimmered in the distance above the water.

The woman turned to face him, her hand in her purse. "I'm sorry," he said again in a whisper. She closed her eyes, then licked his lips. She worked her tongue in deeper into him and, moving it around inside his mouth, worked it deeper as she developed a slight suction with her lips. His eyes closed also, and his head swam with the pulling, moving warmth of her inside him and the engulfing heat outside him.

She pulled the handgun out of her purse.

He leaned into the cool roundness of the barrel that pressed against his belly.

Ya Know What I Mean?

Yesterday, my kid brudder Joey took me ta Yankee Stadium. Until den, I ain't been there since dey fixed it up twenty years ago. Don't ask me why… it's a long story. Anyways, he took me there 'cause he's worried about my blood pressure. He's a smart guy, my kid brudder Joey, he went to the community college downtown.

My old man, he used to bring me to the Stadium alla time. Him and my uncles. They watched them on TV too, drinking Reingolds and yelling "Ya bums!" at the TV. Yeah.

We saw Don Larsen pitch that World Series perfect game in 1956. Yogi run out and jump in his arms. My uncles and my old man -- they went crazy. Last time Jackie Robinson played. Then the Dodgers left Brooklyn. The Giants left too. The bums.

Anyways, like I was saying, they went there to the Stadium and bring me. I remember the Stadium colors: greens and browns -- they ain't there no more. Now, it's all blue – blue all over the joint: blue plastic seats, blue walls.

And that green façade that used to be on the third level? That's gone too. Geez. That's where the Mick hit a ball to right that almost went out. Yeah. Nobody else ever come that close. Nobody. Not even the Babe. The players… said they never heard a sound like that when the ball hit the sweet of the bat. Mel Allen said it was still arcing up; would have gone over 550 feet -- maybe 600.

Yeah. I didn't see that one, but I saw the Mick hit them into the center field bleachers all the time. Now THAT was some shot – 490 feet to the wall over the monuments. Now, they think it's a big deal if they hit one 400 feet. Man.

Anyways, them bleachers, they was wood. Now they ain't got no bleachers in center field there no more; they took them out and painted it all black so's these prima donnas they got now can see the ball at bat. Yeah, ya believe that?

They used to let you exit onto the field. They don't do that no more. My old man and me, we used to stop to look at the monuments after the game… Brass plaques on red granite: Miller Huggins in the middle, Lou and the Babe at the sides. My old man, he had to explain who Miller Huggins was.

Now they moved center field in so's the monuments -- they ain't on the field no more. They fenced them up. Now you got to stand in line to see them. Geez.

Yeah. They used to let you on the field, but not the infield. The guards stood around the infield. My old man talked to one of them. Mighta slipped him a buck – I dunno – so's I could stand behind the plate where Yogi stood. Number 8. Yeah. I stood in his spike marks in the dirt.

And the columns are gone. The kids used to chase foul balls behind the columns where nobody sat. Yeah. No columns no more.

My old man, he used to pay 50 cents for a Ballantine from the vendors, and he bitched 'cause he's paying so much. Now, these fans, they pay five bucks for a beer, and then they throw it. And yesterday, when I was there with my kid brudder Joey, they was throwing beers all over the joint. Five bucks for a beer, and then they THROW it? Geez. My old man, he's turning over in his grave. Yeah.

My kid brudder Joey says I shouldn't get upset about this kinda stuff. He got a calendar with these quotes, the kind you pull one page off each day. Ya know? He gave me one from this guy Maslow, said: "The ability to be in the present moment is a major component of mental wellness."

Like I said, my kid brudder – Joey – he's a smart guy, but he don't know nothing. He don't remember the Stadium the way it used to be…drives a Honda. Ya know what I mean? A BLUE Honda.

Anyways, who is this guy Maslow? And what does he know? Him and my kid brudder Joey.

Yeah.

The Last Time I Saw Her

"Hi Nana…"

She used to bring him coins tied in a knot in her kerchief that she had squirrelled away from his grandfather.

"Hello Alfred!"

Proper Placement

When we were fighting armored vehicles, we set the 40 mm cannon on a rise that faced a bend in the road from whence they would come.

You heard them first, and when they came into view they were headed straight into your sights. There was nothing the lead vehicle could do -- an easy shot. The others were trapped behind.

We used 50 caliber machine guns when fighting airplanes. We knew the Messerschmitt pilots dived out of the sun, so we set up low behind a ridge -- facing the sun. They dove, and we shot some bursts, but did not waste ammo. You can't see the tracers in the bright sunlight anyway.

As they passed low overhead, you saw the pilot's face. We swung the gun around and had them dead in our sights as they rose away. The smart ones banked, but we got them anyway.

Now Anything Goes

They were sitting around a table at the rear of the café.

Newton: Time and space are absolute. I proved that 300 years ago.

Einstein: No longer. We now know that the speed of light is constant regardless of the speed of the source, in which case it is only logical that time and space are variable. Something has to give.

Hemingway: You guys don't know what the fuck you are talking about.

Stein: They made you all a lost generation, Hem.

Hemingway: That was the War. It blew apart all tradition.

Newton: Yes, but thanks to my friend Einstein here you also lost the comfort of stable reference frames.

Einstein: I'm sorry. I had no idea Relativity would have impact outside of the realm of science.

Stein: A rose is a rose is relativism…

Hemingway: Let's order another round.

Catchy Tune

"The girls in France

do the hula-hula dance

and the dance they do

is enough to kill a Jew

and the Jew they kill

is enough to take a pill

and the pill they take

is enough to fry a snake

and the snake they fry

is enough to tell a lie

and the lie they tell

is enough to go to hell"

"Stop singing that song. I'm Jewish."

Manassas

I exited I-95 south, then headed west on the Beltway, I-495. After crossing the Potomac into Virginia, I exited and continued west on I-66.

A sign for the Manassas battlefield rose on the right. I didn't want to go to war, but I wanted to learn about it. So, I pulled into the exit ramp.

The battlefield, close to the highway, was quiet. The lady at the headquarters building said they are closing soon, but the grounds remain open until dark.

Exiting the building, I followed the last tourists out onto the field: They turned left toward the Union cannon lines on the ridge -- following the clockwise self-guided tour. Instead, I turned right along the Confederate lines.

People walked toward me; mostly couples. Husbands, heads down, studied the cannons, looking in them and arguing smooth bore versus rifled bore. Wives looked at the oranging sky and the shadows elongating on the green slopes.

At the end of the Confederate line, I made a left and followed a dirt road down into the hollow between the lines. I climbed the slope toward the Union line.

Two figures approached me as I walked up toward the ridge. The first was tall and thin and wore a bright blue baseball cap. He barely nodded as he went past.

The second man was older and grayer. He had a cane in his left hand and limped with his right elbow sticking out and back. He wore a faded brown baseball cap with a farm-equipment insignia. His stubbled beard moved toothless jaws side to side as he limped down toward me. He stopped in front of me and smiled.

"Ya learnin' anythin' son?" he asked with a soft drawl.

"Sure," I smiled back.

He gazed down the slope at the receding figure. "That there's my grandson," he said. "Always in a hurry." He shook his head, and then looked back at me.

"MY grandfather fought here," he said. He pointed with his cane up at the confederate line, to where Stonewall Jackson earned his sobriquet. "He was with Jackson," he continued. "Got shot in the thigh." He looked again at his grandson, and I thought he would walk on. Instead, he turned back to me.

"Tell you a story my grandfather used to tell," he said. He pointed again up toward the Confederate line. "General Ewing was cussing all over the place, saying Lee gave him orders to do this, and Johnson gave him orders to do that -- he didn't know what to do. Jackson told Ewing, "You just do what I tell you to do." Then Jackson came back to the line and told my grandfather, "I better stay here. It don't do no good to be away from you men too long."

The old man stepped down the slope, then turned back again.

"I'll tell you another story, son," He said. "Before the battle, my grandfather got separated from his outfit. He stopped at a Yankee farmhouse for some water, and the lady there said, 'I don't give no water to no Rebs.' So he went across the road and the lady there gave him water saying 'Take your time.' Pretty soon some Confederate cavalry came hustling through with Yankees on their tail. Grandfather jumped on a horse and they galloped off. That first Yankee lady – see -- she was stupid, see? The second one was smart. She gave my grandfather water to stall him until the Yankees came."

He turned away and limped down the slope.

The Parable of the Edge

At the Edge of the world a man stood gazing into the abyss. His face reflected in the glowing amber haze.

The road to the edge started many years before as a small path winding through bushes and trees in low, rolling hills. As it went, it grew wider, becoming a dirt lane passing green fields with white houses in the distance. The air was clear.

Continuing, the road became rocky and climbed a steep mountain where the soil was washed out by spring rains and the climb difficult going. The man made it to the top, his feet bleeding but his vision clear. He could see far into the distance.

Over the ridge of the mountains, the road was smoother as it declined, but the man had to be careful, sidestepping patches of ice.

Soon the road leveled out in the flatlands beyond the mountain. It became paved: first with rolled gravel mixed with oiled soil, and then with asphalt. It turned to concrete at the point where it met other roads in a maze of traffic lights, yield signs, and stop signs. The man chose the road on the left.

The surrounding terrain disappeared as the road passed through canyons of tall buildings. The buildings were stately, then became slums of abandoned tenements with graffiti-spewed walls, where cobbles paved the road.

The buildings gave way to misty moors. Shadowy figures hovered above the moors, going nowhere.

Ruts were worn in the cobbles from the passage of ancient caravans. The man tried at first not to walk in them, but then he did. The going was easier that way.

Glimpses of barren lunar landscape now could be seen through the mists. The man walked on, the mists becoming thicker and thicker, and brighter and brighter, until, at the Edge, he faced a dense, glowing amber haze.

The man stopped. He wanted to turn back, but couldn't. He hesitated, then stepped off.

He was on a small path, winding through bushes and trees. The air was clear.

Specie

Since ancient times, money has been in the form of hard metals: gold, silver and copper.

In 1933 Roosevelt stopped minting gold coins. Although illegal, people hoarded gold. In 1964, the U. S. stopped minting silver coins. People hoarded silver. In 1982, the U.S. stopped minting copper pennies, and switched to zinc. Now people hoard pre-1982 copper pennies, while the zinc industry lobbies congress to keep minting worthless zinc pennies at a cost of 1.76 cents each.

Coins are bulky -- suitable only for retail transactions; transportable paper money (banknotes) enables large money transactions and fast cash transfer between banks; fractional bank reserves enable credit in multiples above the base money supply that creates even more money; plastic enables fast electronic transactions. Pay Pal… cryptocurrency…dark transactions…

Will people hoard zinc?

Risk Analysis

Known known: You're gonna die.

Known unknown: You don't know when.

Unknown unknown: What then?

Airport

He didn't like airport bars, and here he was sitting in one. The plane was late, but the scotch was good. He took his time: sipping it, looking around at the people: people drinking in the dim lights of the bar or walking out in the fluorescent corridor that had high trussed ceilings. Some passed by on the moving walkway on the far side of the corridor.

At first, he hated them all, but as the scotch took hold he mellowed and felt companionship with them -- suspended, like he was, in time and place. Life on ice.

Ice… He thought of Tucker Smith singing *Cool* against headlights in the garage in *West Side Story*.

He looked down into the glass. The scotch was almost gone. Should he have another? The glow he had was perfect – he didn't want to spoil it.

He ordered another. When it came, he held the glass up against the corridor lights. Pulsating colors refracted through the ice suspended in the amber liquid.

He set the full glass down, paid, got up and walked out into the corridor, singing "play it cool, boy " to himself, and snapping his fingers.

Layered Learning

When you learn guitar, first come chords, then notes. Scales come from notes and progressions come from chords, and, finally, intervals come.

Intervals are spaces between notes in a chord (vertical) or a progression (horizontal). Wide intervals create pleasant feeling. Tight intervals create uneasy feeling: tension needing resolution. Feeling is the object of art.

Practice internalizes memory into the hands. All arts, trades and crafts learn in layers, each built upon the previous:

A painter must practice and master classical techniques of shape, light, form, perspective, color and depth, and then combine those learnings to create art that conveys feeling.

A woodworker learns tools and sharpening, the feel of grain, different wood characteristics, and practices joining to create structural strength without adding unnecessary wood.

A writer practices grammar and reads poetry to learn how to condense meaning – feeling - into words; reads short stories and novels to learn how to create structure, character and plot; and learns a different language to understand syntax (word meaning and order) and appreciate the idioms, oddities and soul of a language; e.g. a unique power of English is its ability to make any noun into a verb: "Xerox that paper!"

Use active voice (passive voice deflects accountability). Shun adverbs. Small paragraphs? Shape the writing. Dylan said words have color -- they also have shape.

Similes. Alliteration. Feel the rhythm of the words to know where to place the different increasing pauses: commas, semicolons and periods. Lincoln used commas effectively (see his *Second Inaugural Speech*).

Play with different tenses, perspectives, *Stream of Consciousness* (interior monologue), and Hemingway's *Iceberg Theory (Theory of Omission*- the deeper meaning of a story should not be evident on the surface). Don't over-describe, it insults the imagination of your reader (George Saunders).

Let it rest. Edit. Rest again. Re-edit. Get the words right (Hemingway).

Good writing doesn't call attention to itself, and language came before writing (*Linguistics: A Modern View of Language*. Henry Lee Smith Jr.)

The point of looking at words is to help us see the world (Michel Dirda on J. L. Austin, the WaPo, January 24, 2024).

Maybe language doesn't just describe our world but creates it." (Adam Kirsh, *The New Yorker*, October 10, 2022).

More on Learning

The first layers are simple. Then they become complex. Then they become simple again as learning is internalized and non-essentials fall away.

Buddies

An early memory is driving with dad out Rt 46 to the Garfield VA hospital to see his war buddy Boo. Boo had brought home a French girl and married her. Soon she left him. His drinking became so bad he had to be hospitalized.

Pete was another buddy. His left hand had been "blown off" in a foxhole -- dad warned me not to say anything. Pete sat with his stub folded under his right hand. He had two beautiful daughters I was in love with.

Years later, mom told me of a reunion where dad joined all his buddies to see "their" Padre. The men laughed in a conference room. Their wives sat smoking in the bar, smoking.

Diminished Chord

The diminished chord is a binding force of music.

The diminished chord, actually a diminished 7th chord, consists of three minor third intervals – 4 notes equally spaced -- stacked upon each other (C diminished is C, Eb, Gb, and A).

This symmetry eliminates internal tension in the chord which allows it to resolve anywhere.

My guitar teacher Harry Leahey told me "When in doubt use a diminished."

(https://www.youtube.com/watch?v=kbPjxAD6b7o)

Freddie

Everyone on the block thought Freddie was funny-looking. His ears stuck out and he had a pointy nose, but big dark eyes stared out under straight black hair that fell over his face. Once he was in an accident, and wore that stupid whiplash thing around his neck that pushed his ears out even more. It was hard to keep a straight face when talking to him.

He lost job after job, and his wife – Nancy -- hated his guts. They'd drink all evening, get loud and start fighting. Someone would call the cops. It became routine for the cops.

Ours was a small narrow street in a gentrifying area of the city. Rowhouses filled such streets, block after block in neighborhoods, each its own little world. Party walls between the houses transmitted voices and noise that fueled next-day gossip.

Parking was on one side of the street. Parking was a territorial imperative. Unless you live in a city you don't understand the life-and-death premium attached to parking spaces, or the consternation caused when an unsuspecting outsider parks on the block.

Our street teed at both ends and so suffered little traffic -- good for kids playing in the summer, but not good in winter because it was not snowplowing priority.

The block could be socked in for days after a major snowstorm, with cars left stranded. Whenever there was a forecast of an impending snowstorm, competition for spaces near the ends of the block, where you could dig out more easily, intensified. Newcomers were caught unaware, as I was that first winter -- when I left our car square in the middle of the block.

The next morning, snow drifted two feet deep. Cars were buried. My wife Gina and I, needing our car for work, called the city: It would take a week before our street would be plowed -- infuriating because the main thoroughfares at both ends of the street were cleared.

We both stayed home that day. That evening, I resolved to shovel our car out. I was in good shape. Besides, neighbors, seeing me work, would come out to help.

"I'm going to shovel the street," I said to Gina.

"What?!"

"You heard me."

"You'll have a heart attack."

I put on light layers. She handed me a shot of brandy: "Here. It'll open up your veins." I downed it in one swig.

And so, I started.

First, I cleared snow from around our car, and stopped to admire my work: a silver island in a sea of white. Then I started working toward the east end of the street, toward the lower drifts. I often couldn't throw the snow, and carried shovelfuls to the sidewalk.

I monitored my heartbeat and stopped to rest after every four shovelfuls. This required willpower: I got into the rhythm of the work, and couldn't let it get ahead of my heart. If you fall into this trap, your heart tries to catch up, and you stop or die.

So, I stopped and leaned on my shovel, gazing up at the clear starlit sky. Neighbors peeked out, but none came out to help. My disgust mounted as I worked my way down the block.

As I neared Freddie's house, he leaned out. His eyes lighted up and he flashed a big smile.

"What the hell you think you're doing? Shoveling the street?" he yelled.

"What's it LOOK like I'm doing?"

Freddie came out wearing a heavy coat and a pom-pom hat pulled down low over his big ears. He carried a shovel.

He dug in beside me and we started making great time. He was happy, and my mood brightened alongside his.

Freddie stopped shoveling. "Hey Nan," he yelled to his wife, who had been watching us through the front window.

She came to the door, "What do you want?"

"Bring us some beers!"

She brought us two bottles. We unscrewed the caps, and drank the beers. The cold beer flowed down my hot insides. One of the best beers I have ever tasted.

We finished the beers, finished the street, and then backed our cars out and put them back in their spaces. Neighbors came out to dig out theirs.

A few months later, after the snow melted, we heard a sound like a firecracker popping, and Nancy came running out into the street, screaming, "Freddie shot himself!"

We collected money, sent flowers, and walked over to Lambruski's Funeral Home to pay our respects.

Years later, after we moved, I read a news article about our old street. There was a photo of Nancy smiling – the caption called her the "Mayor of the Block."

(This story submitted to Loudoun County Public Library, VA short story contest 2/6/2025)

Hands – Part 2

He learned so much from the hands from watching them work.

They had the confident, graceful movement of hands that have spent a lifetime doing a craft: rhythmic, smooth, firm -- yet gentle. He still has the tools he watched the hands use. He often uses them, thus re-establishing his place in the world.

He knew every crack, every scar. Each scar had a story. Some stories had been told him; others, the ones from the war, from handling the big guns, hadn't. He learned about them years later when he read the journals the hands kept during the war. He hadn't been told about the journals, either.

He liked the way the hands cupped the harmonica, opening and closing, feeling the music. With the harmonica, it was more than just the hands; it was whole body playing -- everything moving with the music. He was told was how the hands played *Lili Marlene* for a German prisoner while the prisoner knitted him a hat.

He still has the hat.

The surface of the fingernails of the hands was not smooth like his own. Cracks ran the length of the nails from the cuticle to the tip. The texture of the skin of the fingertips appeared rough to his eyes.He was surprised by their soft touch when they had rubbed dirt on his spider bite to stop him crying.

The hands had greeted him with a smiling, warm, strong handshake, the likes of which he never experienced from any other hands.

He missed the hands so.

Pay Attention to What You Are Doing

To make a robot, I bolted a bulb socket (for the "brain") and an electric motor (to drive the wheels) inside a large tin can. Instinctively, I connected them in a wired loop: one wire of a two-wire electric plug cord to the motor, then the motor to the socket, then the socket back to the remaining wire of the cord.

Without realizing it, I had created a "series" circuit, where the input voltage from the cord was split between the motor and the socket. I plugged it in – everything worked, but the bulb was dim and the motor turned slowly.

Uncle Joe pulled up. "What are you doing?" he asked?

An electrician before he had started working in the textile mills in Paterson, he showed me how to connect one of the wires of both the motor and the socket to one wire of the cord (a three-way connection), and their remaining wires to the other wire of the cord -- thus creating a "parallel" circuit where each item received full voltage.

I messed up the connections.

"Pay attention to what you are doing."

I fixed the connections: The motor ran fast and the bulb shined brightly.

What's It All About?

My dad's name, Mario, led to the nickname "Moe" which he endured but did not like. So, he did not let mom name me Mario after him and they compromised on Alfred, his middle name.

Thus, I became "Little Al" to distinguish me from my older cousin -- "Al" or "Big Al" -- a twin, who also had been named Alfred after my father. Our shared names bonded us. In a picture I am a toddler, and he has a bat over his left shoulder and is biting the nails of his right hand. When I was 12, he died in a street fight. I knelt at his coffin and stared at the rosary beads wrapped around his bitten nails.

Alfred is derived from "Elf-read" which means "Wise Elf" – a good counsellor. In my life Alfred devolved:

"Alfie" after the Bacharach song; "Fred" or "Freddie" from girls who liked me; "Alfonso" from people who teased me; "Alfredo" from Italian-minded friends; and "Al-fart", "Al-freak" or "Al-fuck" from people who disparaged me.

Once I betrayed Alfred: during college summers I worked in a machine shop with a German immigrant, who at the beginning erred by calling me Steve -- my middle name. I didn't correct him; he continued for three years. Finally, he asked me why I let him call me Steve when everyone else called me Al. I shrugged.

By the way, my dad's friends had called me "Little Moe."

Nellie

When I was 7 my grandfather still had a coat factory on the first floor of our apartment building. A large electric motor in the basement ran a leather belt up through the floor to drive a shaft that powered a bank of sewing machines.

Italian ladies at the machines sewed pieces of wool coat fabric. The machines clattered over the ladies' chatter. Large fans in cages on poles circulated wooly air overhead.

Grandpa cut the fabric on a large table. He arranged templates on a fabric sheet, outlined them in chalk and cut around the shapes. Sheet layers underneath created multiple identical pieces that the ladies used in their sewing.

Nellie operated a large ironing press at the back of the shop. He was my first black person. I sat on the elevated threshold of the open doors, listening to him sing *Hey Good Lookin'* and tell me stories about growing up in the south.

The press consisted of two covered ironing boards – a lower board hinged to an opposed upper board that closed like a clam. Nellie maneuvered a coat onto the lower board and closed the upper. Steam hissed out. Sweat and condensation from the steam on his black skin shined -- reflecting yellow from the pendant light fixture hung above.

My friend Tommy lived with his mom and his big brother Buddy in an apartment over the corner stationary store. Tommy didn't talk about his father, and nobody messed with his mom. She wore a bloody white apron behind the meat counter at the A&P.

We hung in an old storage shed behind the diner, where Buddy sang a song to the tune of Reveille:

> There's a nigger in the grass
>
> With a bullet up his ass
>
> Take it out, take it out
>
> Like a good girl scout.

"Nigger" conjured up a hairy animal with sad dark eyes lying wounded in the tall grass. I felt sorry for him, or her, or whatever it was.

Home, dad was at the kitchen table listening to the Yankees on the radio, his hand cupped around his cigarette to hide the glow the way he had learned in the war. He didn't talk about the war, but once he said to me, "I hope you never have to go, Al."

"Hey dad," I said. "Listen to the neat song I learned today." I sang it to him.

"Where did you learn that?" he asked.

"From Buddy."

"Well, that song has a word that hurts Nellie." I knew which word he meant. "You wouldn't want to say anything to hurt Nellie, would you?"

"No sir."

Aunt Jo

Ilmars and I left the school and headed down the Avenue. We ran into Beverly, whom I never had liked. So, I was annoyed when she said "I heard something bad happened to your family." I scoffed, but a bad feeling welled.

The feeling faded as Ilmars and I continued down the Avenue. We went into Luhmann's soda fountain to hang. Stagger Lee played on the juke box. After a while I left out the back entrance.

I walked across the parking lot toward our apartment building. Dad came out: "Your cousin Al was in a fight and it killed him. Your Aunt Jo is in the kitchen. Go in and say how sorry you are."

I hesitated up the steps and went in. Family hovered around the room.

Aunt Jo sat at the table by herself.

First Draft Lottery

In 1969, the Vietnam War was in full swing. To avoid the uncertainties of the draft, you had to enlist. Rink, Doug, Anthony and I had taken the train into New York to take the Navy entry test. Then we waited until December 1.

That evening, we sat around the radio in our off-campus apartment. They started reading the dates: Rink came up first, #19, November 1st; he jumped up and punched a hole in the wall. Anthony came next, #65, May 10; he was quiet.

My birthday did not come up until #275; Doug's #320. We were in the clear: They wouldn't be taking anyone over #200.

Doug and I went to grad school. Rink and Anthony joined the Coast Guard – a longer hitch but safer than the Navy.

2nd Amendment

The establishment of distant colonies in the new hemisphere, facilitated by the Age of Enlightenment, enabled a unique self-government to form there.

The resulting U.S. Constitution, written in a place and time that contained the last vestige of slavery that had existed throughout history, contained the basis not only for eliminating that slavery, but also for creating the best (according to Franklin, in spite of its inherent flaws) possible structure of government that balanced individual liberty vs. the common good: "A republic if you can keep it."

However, that document contained the seed of its own destruction: a single sentence Second Amendment with poorly placed commas.

Dick Street

In 1954, while my grandfather renovated our apartment building, we moved out temporarily. My dad, a vet, got us into housing the government had built for returning vets on Dick Street, next to the railroad tracks. Many kids lived there.

We snuck an ax from the shed and chopped branches off discarded Christmas trees to make lances. We formed opposing lines to charge each other and take jabs in the gut. That really hurt.

Jimmy was the oldest kid. He had a kid sister Judy.

Across Columbia Avenue there was a ball field with trees along the tracks where we hung out and lit fires in a hollowed out old tree. In the fall when the grass was dry a flame jumped out of the tree and set the field afire. We hid and watched the fire trucks come.

Before the fire event happened, we were hanging by the hollowed tree and Jimmy challenged us to show our pee-pees. So, there we were, standing in a circle with our pee-pees hanging out.

Judy wanted to show hers too but Jimmy wouldn't let her.

Times Square

We caught the 167 bus: fifty cents each took us through Teaneck, Ridgefield Park, the Lincoln tunnel and into Port Authority bus terminal.

From the terminal we walked east along 42nd Street. A couple guys bought stiletto knives at a shop next to Ripley's Believe It or Not.

Then we turned left at 7th Avenue and walked up to 46th and Broadway. If you hung at that corner long enough, men came and offered you $10 to let them give you a blow job.

I left the guys at the corner, walked into the Square, and sat at the base of the George M. Cohan statue.

Yankee Doodle Dandy…

Doodle - mom used to call my prick "your doodle bug." I didn't want some guy sucking my doodle bug.

The Camel man blew smoke rings from the billboard above.

Years Later…

…a guy followed me into the men's room in Cornell's Olin library. He sidled up to the urinal next to mine and looked down at my dick. His shaking hand reached out a $10 dollar bill.

I shook my head, zipped up, and walked out.

Bailey Hall

Bailey Hall at Cornell is a Greek revival rotunda with a portico entrance atop a monumental staircase. A plaza extends out from the base of the staircase. I went there one summer evening to see Pete Seeger perform.

The show was stopped soon after it started. Pete said "The fire marshal says we have exceeded the capacity of the building," and told us to go out front, where he would continue the performance.

Pete and his banjo moved around in front of the columns at the top of the stairs. We sat cross-legged in the plaza, and sang *Wimoweh* under the starlit sky.

283

The '57 Chevy pulled up next to me at the light. The guy looked over: A challenge.

I knew the '57 had a 283 cubic-inch engine. I wasn't sure of its horsepower, but knew it was well under 300. My '67 GTO had 400 c.i. with 330 h.p. The guy didn't have a chance… if I could keep it on the ground.

The GTO had a 4-speed Hurst shifter on the floor with a heavy clutch. If I let it out too fast in first, it burned rubber and fish-tailed.

I hesitated, but Ralph, in shotgun, whispered "Take it." So, I nodded back to the guy in the 283.

The light changed. I eased out. The 283 jumped ahead.

The tires grabbed. I nailed it, slammed into second and shot out front.

I blew the guy's doors off.

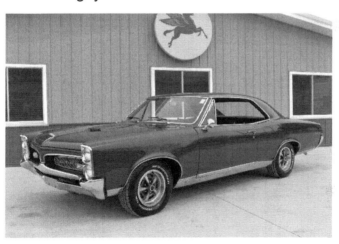

Elmer

When we first met Ilmars, he was wearing a black cowboy hat and riding his tricycle in the parking lot behind Connie's Hobby Shop. He said his name was Ilmars, but we heard it as "Elmer." We called him Elmer for years. He didn't seem to mind.

He had blond hair and blue eyes. My father took a film of us playing cowboys, shooting toy guns in a wooden fort. I am wearing my Davy Crockett outfit. Elmer is wearing his cowboy hat, a plaid shirt and a red bandana.

Elmer lived in an apartment on Washington Avenue. I spent many sleep-overs there. We wrestled on the floor.

Elmer was a better baseball player. I couldn't field ground balls -- he was a natural.

We attended Washington School together, but in fourth grade Elmer transferred to Franklin School. We drifted apart.

We re-connected in high school. I called him Ilmars. He laughed his way down the halls with Joe and Charlie. I hung with Ritchie and Artie. Ilmars was a good bowler and started smoking.

After high school, I got a student deferment, a high lottery number, and went to grad school. Elmer went into the Navy to avoid the draft, then he drove a tractor trailer truck, got married and had children.

Elmer was the only boy I ever kissed.

My Right Side

My right ear doesn't equalize pressure. It hurts when I dive and also when I descend in an airplane. Decongestants, gum, and jaw stretches do not help. It clogs, and I am partially deaf. Hours later I sneeze or cough, it pops, and I can hear again. I think the eustachian tube is bent.

After college I worked in a mechanical room near high-pitched centrifugal chillers. Right ear ringing started that continues to this day.

Vision in my right eye is worse than the left. I have stigmatism and floaters there and "retinoschisis" – fraying at the edges of the retina, causing bleeding and laser surgery.

The teeth on the left side of my mouth are aligned. I have always chewed on that side.

My eyetooth sticks out of my right side. My parents couldn't afford braces. I smiled crooked so mom wanted it pulled. She took me to Dr. Keitur's on the Avenue, whose office was in Elmer's old apartment.

The familiarity of the room juxtaposed with my sitting in a dental chair -- mouth full of Novocain -- watching mom and dentist argue whether to pull my tooth.

Dr. Keitur prevailed: tooth removal would destroy the structure of my mouth. I still have the eye tooth. It still sticks out. I remain physically and emotionally attached to it.

The lower jaw canine that opposes this eye tooth never erupted. It is submerged horizontally in the bone, creating a lump that my tongue plays with.

I bite a web of skin on the inside my right cheek. It bleeds; I taste the blood. This web does not exist in my left cheek.

My back hurts on my right lower lumbar side when I sit or stand a long time. If I sleep on my right side the pain comes, so I favor sleeping on my left side.

The left side of my brain has made me strong at math. I have a graduate engineering degree.

I have minimal artistic creativity which originates on the right side.

Arthur

The summer of 1965, after I graduated from high school, before I started at Rutgers, I worked as a locker room boy at Alpine Country club. Alpine is off Route 9W not far from the George Washington bridge, so many New York celebrities were members.

Arthur ran the locker room. He had slight lisp, often had wet used towels draped over his shoulder, hustled for tips, and made book for members who wanted to play the ponies.

We worked in a small room off the main locker room. A pay phone hung on the wall, and a work bench had two rotating electric wheels: one with a cloth buffer that we used to polish members' street shoes that were left in front of lockers while they were out on the links; the other with wire brushes to clean their golf-shoe spikes when they went into the showers.

Once I was cleaning spikes while Peter Falk was arguing on the phone. A car beeped outside. Peter ordered: "Hey kid -- go move my car." His black Lincoln Continental was left running with the door open, blocking the driveway. I maneuvered it into a space. It steered like a boat.

Another time, I polished Ed Sullivan's shoes and cleaned his alligator-skin spikes. He had small feet.

The locker room was split in two sections separated by a door: Ed and I were alone -- he was in the other room. I went to the door to say hello. He was sitting hunched on the bench, his back to me and his head in his hands. I did not disturb him.

Arthur had built a wood lattice was over the concrete floor in our work room -- I asked him why:

"You ever stand on concrete all day?" he lisped.

Drips

I am tired of peeing down my leg. Whether I pull, shake, or stretch it, drips roll down my leg inside my pants. So, I drop my pants and wash my leg. If my clothes have piss, I change.

When I was young, I would just shake it a few times, compress my bladder, and tuck it away: all automatic.

Now they tell me that continuing to compress my bladder will cause lost elasticity and a serious problem. So, I no longer compress… still I pull… shake…stretch… No avail. Still drips.

Now the automatic is gone. Reflex is gone too. When you are young you do stuff by reflex that's taken for granted. Like walking down stairs. Run down them -- not a second thought. Now there's hesitation. Plan ahead. Grab the rail.

Which foot do I use first?

Johnstown

In August 1977 I was with FEMA cleaning up and repairing the aftermath of the third Johnstown flood. The heights of the previous floods of 1889 and 1936 were marked on buildings downtown.

I escaped the front-end loaders removing debris and the body bags lined up in the high school gym by driving up Little Conemaugh [the South Fork] River hollow to see the [South Fork] dam that caused the '89 flood, the worst of the three.

A platform overhangs the area of the dam break -- the jagged outline of the break remains below. The dam had gone in the middle of the night, creating a wall of water that rushed down the hollow, sweeping wood houses, barbed wire and sleeping people down through the town.

On the far side of the town, past where the confluence of Little Conemaugh and Stoney Creek [South Fork] forms the Conemaugh, a stone arched railroad bridge had dammed up debris to form a heap with people trapped inside. Fire ignited from oil lamps. Screams continued for three days.

I drove back down the hollow. The radio announcer said Elvis died. *Love Me Tender* came on.

July 4, 2010

I lay half-awake. Our cat, Katy-bit, ran up the stairs and hid under our bed.

A glow shimmered behind her, so I got out of bed, rounded the corner, and faced raging orange flames outside our third-floor bedroom window.

Jackie lay asleep, her face peaceful in the glowing light. I roused her and dragged her half-asleep by the arm downstairs.

Smoke got thicker and thicker as we descended. We made it to the front door with smoke so thick we could hardly breathe. A key was in the dead-bolt lock -- I grabbed it, opened the door, and came face to face with our neighbor Marc, who had been pounding on the door.

Three Rules

1. Conserve principal
2. Make small changes
3. Use Time to make corrections

Lake Being

Our canoe glided through lily pads close to shore. Dragonflies rose from the pads, hovered in the still air, and then darted off at right angles. Bright sunlight reflected off the mirrored lake surface that was broken by the motion of the canoe and the infrequent dipping of our paddles. Startled perch shot out from weeds in the clear water under the shadow of the canoe.

A breeze rippled the water out in the open lake. Further out, stronger wind drove the water, making the lake surface rougher. Years earlier when we had first started canoeing, we fought the natural motion of a lake, trying to go where it did not want us to go. Soon we learned to let it take us where it wanted us to go.

Lakes often seem to have no beginning, but they always have an end. A lake always took us to the end, usually a small, still cove, lily pads and reeds growing in the shallows. Animals and fish gather there where food collects in abundance.

Discoveries awaited at the end. We drifted in the pads and the reeds, and waited, into the twilight, for animals to come.

Once, after we had waited a while, a big blue bird with a long, curved neck alit in the shallows nearby to fish in the reeds. Touching the paddles to the water, hardly breathing, we drifted within a few feet before it arced its wings and moved to another spot. Again, we approached, and again it moved. The third time, the bird tired of the game and flew up into a tall pine tree at the edge of the lake and sat there, watching us.

Another time, when it was almost dark, a moose came out of the trees and waded into the shallows. Weeds hung from its jowls as it drank from the lake and looked up into our eyes, focusing for a moment, ears twitching, deciding whether to be alarmed. Again, we hardly breathed.

The moose put its nose down again, finished drinking, turned and lumbered back into the trees.

When darkness came, we paddled out of the cove and back up the lake under the big stars of the summer Vermont sky. Bats swooped down. Sequins reflected off the lake. It was then that we felt at one with the Lake.

But in Vermont they call them ponds.

Ultimate Reality?

We observe and interact with particular things in the world around us, but we think in universals.

We arrive at universals in our minds by abstracting non-essentials from the particular things we observe, and we sort them into categories. Thus, we organize the world so we can deal with it.

This leads to a question: If humans were not present on the earth, would universals exist? (If a tree falls in the woods, and nobody is there to hear it, does it make a sound?). What remains? A random world of particulars?

Debate has gone on for three thousand years: Which is the ultimate reality -- Particulars in the world (skeptics), universals in our heads (theology), or the relationship of the two (science)?

Poem Writer

If I could be completely free
a poem writer I would be.

I'd look into the soul of me
and deep within what truth I'd see?

I'd listen to what people say
and probe for meaning's underplay;

their wasted words discarded first
from concentrated lines of verse.

Like Kilmer write of lovely trees
and read the great philosophies.

And rage in dirges at the war
which seems to come forever more.

But awe at mountains everywhere
and wonder if gods do dwell there.

And watch a woman turn her face
a lovely curvature in space.

But who am I to try to be,
what I know I cannot. See?

La Mia Ora Speciale

Dopo molti anni ho trovato un buon amico nel mare. C'e' un'ora molto particolare per me, una combinazione di momenti che io chiamo "l'ora bassa" che mi fa apprezzare questo mare che ho sempre amato: il tramonto del sole e la marea bassa.

Durante il tardo pomeriggio estivo, il sole rende le ombre lunghe e sottile. Queste ombre si rincorrono sopra la superficie onulata della sabbia che si appiana prima di incontrarsi con l'acqua, dove le forme ondolate cominciano a giocare con i movimenti ondosi del mare.

Quando la marea e' bassa, le onde non sono molto grande; quasi delicatamente toccano la sabbia liscia che a poco a poco diventa ondulata. A parte il rumore ritmico delle onde, tutto diventa silenzioso perche', a quest'ora, non ci sono molte persone sulla spiaggia. Si vedono solo alcune famiglie in cui i genitori, seduti, si parlano, ed I bambini, con un silenzio non caratteristico, si diventono piacevolmente nella zona dove le onde del mare arrivano e poi spariscono dentro la sabbia.

Poco oltre i pescatori gettano le loro lunghe canne da pesca al di la' delle onde -- verso l'orizzonte, dove i gabbiani volteggiano in grandi archi.

A volte rimango sulla spiaggia fino a che la luce del sole scompare all'orizzonte e la luna appare come una faccia grande che riflette la luce arancione del sole. Tutto ad un tratto il cielo diventa scuro a parte la luna e le luce delle stelle.

In questo momento, quando la luna si riflette sul mare, incomincio a camminare ed il riflesso di questa luce quasi irreale sembra mi segue

In Cerca di Michelangelo

"Nella camera le donne vengono e vanno, parlando di Michelangelo…."

Non e' molto difficile descrivere la sensazione che si prova nel vedere direttamente un capolavoro di Michelangelo. Ricordo bene la mia prima volta, quando vidi la Pieta' a New York durante la "Worlds Fair" del 1964. L'effetto della luce sulla bella delicate della Madonna, nonstante il fatto che avessi potuto ammirarla solo per 30 secondi, rimane ancor oggi nella mia memoria.

E' un po' piu' difficile descrivere la sensazione di restare solo con una delle sue meravigliose opera, il che ha piu' forza quando accade improvvisamente. La mia prima occaisione di sperimento fu durante il mio primo viaggio in Italia, mentre passeggiavo da solo per le strade di Roma. In una strada larga vidi una grossa chiesa dall'aspetto molto elegante, davanti a cui scorrevano rapidamente numerose Fiat. Allora non lo sapevo, ma si trattava della Chiesa di Santa Maria Sopra Minerva: una chiesa fatta costruire da una papa sulle rovine di un vecchio tempio romano dedicato alla dea della sapienza. Entrai in questa chiesa non so perche', forse cercavo solo di fuggire dalla noia della strada di fuori. Tutt'ad un tratto fui colpito dal grande silenzio e dal buio all'interno della chiesa.

Mi avvicinai alla sagrestia. Li' solo riconobbi immediatamente una scultura del Cristo Risorto, opera di Michelangelo. Aveva un corpo molto atletico ma un viso molto dolce, quasi femmineo, molto vulnerabile, e che allo stesso tempo sembrava indicare conoscenza delle sofferenze di tutta l'umanita'. Non aveva nel viso quella stessa espressione che avevo visto nei libri di storia dell'arte.

Il giorno dopo, a Roma, andai alla Cappella Sistina. Invece di osservare tutto il soffito nella sua magnificenza, il mio squardo mise a fuoco il volto della sibilla Delfica. Prima quello stesso giorno avevo visto quello stesso volto nella scultura di Rachele accanto a Mose' nella Chiesa di San Pietro in Vincoli. Nella sua faccia Michelangelo volle rappresentare la bellezza universal della sapienza femminile, una rappresentazione simile al volto della Madonna che avevo visto in America molto tempo prima.

Dopo tre giorni a Roma, andai a Firenze. Passeggiare nelle stesse vie di Michelangelo in questa citta' per me e' un vero tuffo nel passato. Fu la sua citta', ed oggi non e' molto cambiata da quell tempo, a parte per le automobile e i modi di vestire della gente.

Andai all'Accademia per vedere il suo David, ma il mio sguardo non rimase a lungo su questo lavoro. Invece fui attratto dale sculture iniziate e non finite. Una specialmente, Lo Schiavo Morente, cercando invano di emergere dalla pietra, creo' per me una visione della forza umana universal, imprigionata nella sofferenza eterna.

Avevo volute andare a Milano alla fine del mio viaggio per vedere l'ultimo capolavoro di Michelangelo, La Pieta' Rondanini, ma non ebbi tempo. Le riproduzioni di questo capolavoro che avevo visto nei libri di storia dell'arte mi avevano colpito per la vera forza del genio maturo di Michelangelo. Allo stesso modo dello Schiavo Morente, la faccia di questo Cristo emerge dalla pietra, ma piu' scuro, l'immagine di qualcuno che sta perdendo la volonta' di vivere. La sua gamba, troppo lunga, sproporzionata, ed il braccio isolato dal corpo, insieme danno una sensazione come d'interruzione del flusso della vita attraverso il corpo morente.

Anni dopo, finalemente ho potuto andare a Milano, al Castello Sforza, per vedere questo suo ultimo lavoro. Era piu' piccolo di che ho immaginato quando l'ho visto nei libri di storia di arte, ma vedere direttamente questa differenza lo da piu' pieta'.

Made in the USA
Middletown, DE
06 July 2025

10185282R00045